Published by Hearts and Crafts, Inc. Long Beach, California
Printed in Taiwan
ISBN: 0-9617072-0-8

BUNNIDUK

AND THE
MERRY MUTTKINS

By Barbara Bullen

ILLUSTRATED BY
Betty Bullen

PUBLISHED BY HEARTS AND CRAFTS • LONG BEACH, CALIF.

One time, not so long ago, there was a beautiful little rabbit named Betty Jane Bunny. She lived in a place called Carrot Corner, in a big beautiful meadow with lots of trees and ponds.

Betty Jane's best friend was a dapper young duck named Arfur Dooner Duck, but his friends just called him Dooner. Betty Jane and Dooner were so crazy about each other that they spent all day every day playing together, and they always dreaded the moment when their parents would call them home for dinner.

Betty Jane's mom, Amanda Bunny, didn't like her daughter having a duck as a best friend. When Betty Jane brought Dooner home with her for dinner one night, she said, "Arfur Dooner, you go straight home and eat with your duck family. I'm not going to smell up my whole burrow by cooking a fish for you!" Dooner tried hard not to let Betty Jane see his tears as he waddled up the burrow tunnel and skampered home.

After he left, Betty Jane's father, P.W., turned to her and said, "Why can't you find some nice bunny friends to play with? What do you see in that duck anyway?"

"D-A-D-D-Y", said Betty Jane, "I like Dooner because he's Dooner, not because he's a duck!" She was very upset but didn't say much because she was such a good little bunny, she would never talk back to her parents. Besides, she was afraid they wouldn't let her play with Dooner anymore.

Dooner had the same problem when he got home and found his mother, Happy Duck, waiting for him. "Arfur Dooner!" said Happy, "Why are you so late getting home?"

"Well, er . . ." stammered Dooner, "I went over to Betty Jane's house for dinner, but her mother sent me home."

"Well, I should say so!" said Happy Duck. "Mercy gracious, they'd probably expect you to eat carrots!" Happy didn't know it, but Dooner had loved carrots ever since the first time Betty Jane gave him one, and he would have preferred them to the fish stew Happy served for dinner that night.

After dinner Dooner's father, Pappy Duck, said "Beverly and Virginia came over to see you today, Dooner. They're such fine young ducks. Why don't you go and visit them tomorrow?"

"Well, maybe," said Dooner. But he knew he wouldn't, because he had promised to teach Betty Jane to swim.

The next day, bright and early, Betty Jane packed a picnic lunch and hurried out of the house before Amanda and P.W. woke up. She went to the little pond where she and Dooner always met. Dooner was already there enjoying an early morning swim. He waved to her as he swam by. Then he spent twenty minutes showing off. "What a wonderful swimmer he is," thought Betty Jane. "If only I could swim like that!"

They spent all day at the pond while Dooner taught Betty Jane to swim. She was really very good. She had nice big feet, and with Dooner there she wasn't afraid at all. "This is so much fun," said Betty Jane. "I don't know why all bunnies don't learn to swim." When they finally got out of the pond, she said, "Now that I can swim, Dooner, you really must learn to hop!"

"Uh, oh," thought Dooner. He wasn't sure he could hop at all with his little web feet, but he was determined to try. After all, Betty Jane had become a fairly good swimmer. So he tried . . . and do you know what? He was a good little hopper!

Betty Jane and Dooner spent many summers hopping and swimming and just loving life. Finally, one summer Dooner got down on his little knees (which, by the way, wasn't very easy for a duck) and asked Betty Jane to marry him. "Of course I will," said Betty Jane. They were so happy. They ran off to tell their parents.

Well, as you might have guessed, Amanda and P.W. and Happy and Pappy were not one bit pleased! P.W. and Pappy decided to separate Betty Jane and Dooner and put a stop to this foolishness forever! They would send Dooner off to the Naval Duck Academy where they all agreed he would be taught proper duck ways.

But the night before Dooner was supposed to leave, he sneaked out of the house and flew over to Betty Jane's house, woke her up, and they ran away together in the middle of the night.

They spent a very long time walking, and when it got light they found themselves in a pretty little green meadow. "How pretty this place is," said Betty Jane. "Let's stay here." Dooner scouted around and found a little pond close by and a wise old owl—who married them that very day. Betty Jane proceeded to dig a nice little burrow hole under a beautiful old tree.

They were so very happy there. Of course they missed their parents a great deal, but they loved each other so much that they stayed in their own little home.

Well, one spring Betty Jane and Dooner had their very own little boy! He had Betty Jane's ears and tail and Dooner's bill and feet. He had little wings under his long ears. He quacked when he was hungry, and he wiggled his little nose (which was really the end of his bill) when he was happy. He could run like a bunny and swim like, well, like a little duck. And he could fly!

Betty Jane and Dooner could have burst with pride. They named him Bunniduk, and they loved him to pieces. What an extraordinary little boy! Bunniduk was the happiest kid in the whole world! He loved his parents, and he spent his days playing and being good and growing up. How wonderful life was!

When Bunniduk was five, Betty Jane and Dooner had a talk. "You know he should be with children his own age," said Dooner.

"I know," said Betty Jane. "I just hoped it wouldn't happen so soon. I guess it's time we moved back." That night they told Bunniduk they were going to move to a place called Carrot Corner and that he would have lots of little friends to play with and grandparents to love him.

Early the next morning they set out on their long journey back to the big meadow. Bunniduk had never been on a trip before and he loved it. He hopped and flew ahead and swam in every puddle and stream they came to. When they finally got to Carrot Corner, who should they run into first but Amanda Bunny.

"Oh, lands sake!" she said. "It's Betty Jane!" She was so happy to see her daughter that she forgot to be mad. She even welcomed Dooner with open arms. "And who's this?" Bunniduk had been hiding behind Dooner.

Betty Jane and Dooner stood proudly as Bunniduk looked up at his grandmother for the first time. "This is our little boy, Bunniduk."

"Well, my goodness." said Amanda. "He's adorable, he looks just like you, Betty Jane, and I love him!" Bunniduk was delighted with himself. He was going to like others. That night they all had dinner with Happy and Pappy Duck. After dinner, P.W. bounced his grandson on his knee and tickled his little webbed feet. Bunniduk was a big hit with his grandparents.

The next day he and his parents went to find a spot of their own. When they got settled, Bunniduk went to the pond for a swim. There were several young ducks playing and swimming around. He jumped right in and swam up and said, "Hi, my name is Bunniduk. Can I play with you?"

"Bunniduk?!" said the biggest duck. "What's a bunniduk? You're just about the funniest looking duck I ever saw!" All the other ducks looked at Bunniduk and laughed. Bunniduk was devastated. The tears flew down his little beak, and he swam, hopped and flew all the way home crying.

He was so upset that Betty Jane and Dooner couldn't understand a thing he said. They finally calmed him down enough to hear what happened. Betty Jane was so sad. It was hard to believe the other children could be so mean. "That's o.k. honey," she said. "It might take awhile for them to accept you, but you must always remember you are a beautiful little boy, inside and out!"

Well, when Bunniduk tried to be friends with the bunnies, they thought he was just as funny as the ducks had. So he spent the rest of that summer hiding from the kids (and their parents) and mostly just playing alone all the time.

One day, after being totally humiliated by a bunch of little girl bunnies, Bunniduk ran off into the forest for a good cry. He wandered off farther than usual, because he couldn't see where he was going for the tears. After a little while he heard the funniest noise. ". . . Ri-bet . . . arf, ri-bet . . . arf, ri-bet . . . arrrrrrf." He opened his eyes and saw the strangest thing he had ever seen. It was a green dog with big frog eyes!

"Who are you?" said Bunniduk.

"I'm Froggie-doggie," said the creature, "and no one will play with me because I'm, well . . . uh, unique looking." Bunniduk could see this creature was upset because he was crying tears the size of lily pads. All of a sudden Bunniduk understood.

"I think you look swell," said Bunniduk. "I'll be your friend." And with that Froggie-doggie's tears changed to smiles, and the two of them went swimming together. They had so much fun playing that Bunniduk was late getting home for dinner. His parents were worried, but when he told them about Froggie-doggie, they weren't mad. Betty Jane and Dooner remembered a time when they were very young. They smiled and told Bunniduk that he should invite Froggie-doggie over so that they could get to know him.

After that day Bunniduk and Froggie-doggie were the best of friends. They spent all their time playing together and having fun. Bunniduk even forgot about how badly the other young ducks and bunnies had treated him.

One day Bunniduk and Froggie-doggie wandered back into the forest to play. When they were not far from where they had met, they heard a whole lot of strange but happy sounds. Soon they came upon the funniest-looking animal either one of them had ever seen. She had antlers and a pointed tail with big cheeks and tiny little ears. "What's your name?" asked Bunniduk.

"Crocopotamoose," she said, "and these are my friends, Piggie-pine, Pelicat and Koalawallaby." Well, they all began to play together. Everyone was so nice and, my goodness, so talented. They came out of the forest and began to meet every day at the little pond. Everyone could swim except Piggie-pine and they were working on her. They had so much fun, they decided to call themselves the Merry Muttkins.

And so the summer went . . .

Soon, some of the kids from town saw them playing. A cute little bunny named Nicole and her friend Evan, the Duck, came to play with them. Well, the Merry Muttkins all remembered how they had been treated when they first came to town and they said, "Why don't you two get lost?! You would never let us play with you, so why should we let you play with us?" Nicole and Evan ran home. Their feelings were hurt very badly.

Bunniduk felt awful . . . so awful that he decided to call a meeting of all the Merry Muttkins. "Do you remember how bad we felt when nobody would play with us?" They all hung their heads. They were so ashamed! They decided to elect Bunniduk and Froggie-doggie to go apologize.

They found Nicole and Evan not too far away playing leapfrog with Nicole's little brother, Matthew. "Er . . . we just wanted to say we're sorry for being so mean. You can play with us anytime you want to."

"Really?" said Nicole.

"Sure," said Froggie-doggie. "Why don't we start by teaching you the *right* way to play leap-frog." They played together all afternoon.

The next day Nicole, Evan and Matt came with some more friends to play with the Merry Muttkins. Pretty soon, everyone was having so much fun playing and learning what each and every one of them could do, why, there was no time to make fun of each other. They were too busy!

Well, the grown-ups learned a lot from their children too. They found out that they could all have more fun and be happier by accepting everyone. Carrot Corner became a place where all creatures could live together no matter what they looked like, or where they came from.

And you know what? *Everyone* lived happily ever after.

The End

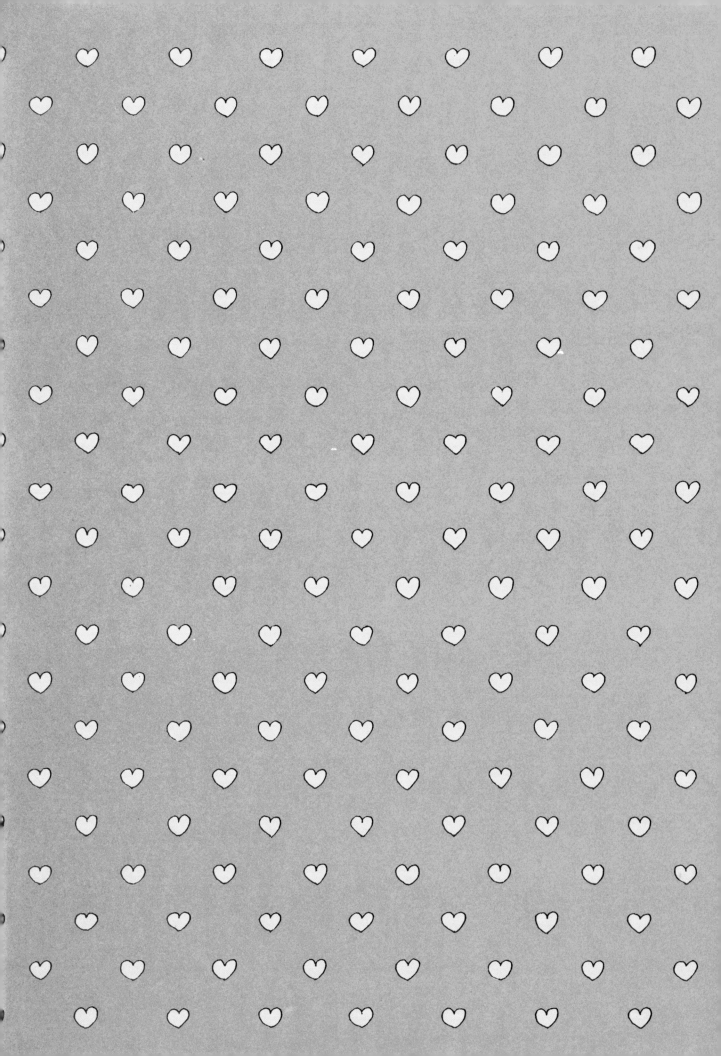